CW00666245

Nothing Burns Like Time

The Félidés Clan

Jae Greyn

Published by Jae Greyn, 2023.

This is a work of fiction. Similarities to real people, places, or events are entirely coincidental.

NOTHING BURNS LIKE TIME

First edition. July 21, 2023.

Copyright © 2023 Jae Greyn.

ISBN: 979-8223049418

Written by Jae Greyn.

Table of Contents

Acknowledgments

Thank you to Sharon, who was willing to give this story a chance and is always ready to read. And to Luc, for your patience.

Dear Reader,

This book is not a love story. There is no HEA, here. In the rest that follow, there are HFN and HEA. This is the beginning of a battle between the goddess of Time, Gi, and Justice and War of Gemini. That's the big one. The smaller ones? It pits brother against brother and majick against majick.

This is dark urban fantasy. There is blood, guts and gore. There is foul language, smoking, and drinking. This involves Plane hopping and time manipulation. It involves parents treating their kids like crap. It involves the death.

Syra is the honorary grandmother of Gemini's children. There is no mpreg. Raven and Scot are Bisexual. Raven is in love with Cyan, who is male.

This is the beginning, and I hope, if you stick around after the trigger warnings, you enjoy it.

Jae

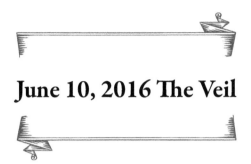

June 10, 2016 The Veil

Raven Lux Félidés, Justice of Gemini
The graduates of Geriden's University were in rare form on the dancefloor as they celebrated. I stood in the office, watching the revelry below through the one-way glass. Between the L and the C of the Veil Club painted in Gothic lettering, I spotted my twin at the bar, talking to an auburn haired young man with beautiful green eyes.

"My Raven, you should at least listen to what they have to say," Syra called from the scrying mirror on my desk. The Source of All Things couldn't work a cellphone, so we communicated the old-fashioned way.

I turned and arched a brow. "Didn't I write the laws they follow?"

"You did." Her amber gaze flickered to green as she fiddled with her thick rope braid of blood-colored hair. She was beautiful, and very mated to the god Famine. Once upon a time, she'd been a flickering thought in my head. She wanted love, and I couldn't promise her that.

"What is the purpose of speaking to the idiots you created after me? None of them talk to me about anything, and I still do their jobs. They don't help me. Why should I help them? One of them has a demi-doodah who frequents my club, and is thrown out at least once a week. If I hadn't put an age limit on attendees for the night, he'd be limping to his car as we speak. If you remember, you told me not to kill him."

"Darling, forget Jer. He is stupid, but he's not the issue. James is a problem. He has them all thinking he's you and is trying to rewrite our laws."

"Yes, and when he goes too far, people end up here looking for a job. I'm winning the war and the only blood spilled is the damn demitasse Jer."

"Demitasse?"

"Half-assed, half-full, half the god." I grinned.

She laughed and then cleared her throat. "Do be serious. James has done something really bad that will affect us all, my Raven. I don't know what, yet."

"What do I have to do to judge this person? Couldn't I summon him here◈"

"No, my darling. He is Chaos' grandson. To obliterate the pretender, you'd have to be born to take his majick."

"I don't need his majick. I have enough." And trouble, too. Syra didn't know what she asked.

Born Vessels needed to feed. They needed mates. They needed to eat and sleep.

I only had to feed when I was hurt. Eating and sleeping wasn't a requirement. As for the mate part, well. Scot and I were identical from the roots of our black hair to the soles of our feet and no one could tell us apart. Anyone who'd smelled like a goodnight for me, ended up in his bed.

He had a four step program, too. The first was dinner and a kiss at the door. The second? Flowers the next morning, and they took him to the movies that night. The third? Jewelry. Scot dated rich men searching for a mate. The fourth, if he liked them enough not to grill them, he fucked them. If not, he gave them a beautiful memory, and sent them home happy, never seeing them again.

We smelled good to everyone, so he played them. The God of War was a player and bored with the game.

I'd met someone, a beautiful someone with champagne blond hair, cyan eyes, and the most spectacular smile. We'd spent the day together after a fight in the alley behind my hotel. He prayed and I went. He was taking his brother's duty for the day, and had never killed a Vampire before.

He lived in The Garden with Syra, so I couldn't send him home. We spent the rest of the day together and I was snared by his quick wit, quiet sighs, and most kissable lips. The best part? He hadn't met Scot. Cyan was my secret and I didn't want to lose him.

Syra wanted me to give him up and agree to birth, to clean up a mess made by the other gods?

I didn't want that. I wanted Cyan.

The prayer pounding against my temples breached several layers of spelled titanium to reach me, drawing me from my thoughts. I held my hand up and cocked my head to the side. "I'll call you back."

It took me five minutes to find her, and I counted spaces to the restroom. A blond head bowed over the neck of a female with green eyes and long red hair. She reached a hand out to me, and I took it, placing the other on the back of the man's head, jerking him away and breaking his neck. It wouldn't kill him, but he'd stay down while I healed her.

I'm Sonny, and that is not my dad, she thought as I tore my wrist and poured blood into the chunk of flesh she was missing from her neck.

The man stirred, taking out my knee, and slamming my head into the mirror. I counted spaces to the alley behind the club, dragging him with me.

The glass tinkled to the pavement in a shrill sound, making my temples throb.

Muddy brown eyes overlaid Tiger blue as the Essence wobbled in the Vessel, a Vessel identical to another employee. The Bear didn't fit into a Tiger suit. The bad Syra spoke of had happened, and in my own club.

Ceael Felins, one of my own men, was dead.

The smell of mothballs permeated the man's flesh, missing the hint of copper carnations that accompanied Human Vampires.

Either way, my opponent was just as deceased.

Blow for blow, we were evenly matched because the dead man felt no pain and popped the bones into place again. I'd ripped his throat open first, and my claws gripped his heart, but he'd stopped me with a move I hadn't counted on. My sword.

It sliced clean through me as if I was a stick of butter.

"I'm James, grandson of Chaos, you demishit. I own you now." His fangs glistened under the harsh street light, and I gave him one second to savor his victory.

With a shaky hand, I wrapped my fingers around the hilt and staggered back. Hot blood filled my mouth, and removing the spelled titanium took every ounce of strength I had left. It was slow going, and metal scraping bone jarred my teeth.

The colors-those snarky shits that were my eyes, ears, and memory keepers-winked out one by one. The walls no longer glowed green, the handprints on the brick no longer glowed yellow, and the wiring and waterlines no longer glowed blue and red.

"Only a god can sustain a god, and only a mate can wield your weapons." The Source's words competed with the hum of the blade feeding from my existence.

The majick was in the blood, and the Sword of Justice answered to that. Green apples wafted towards me from the handle- the scent of a summer's sunrise on the beach only in want of a good cup of coffee. Lips curved into a spectacular smile, head thrown back in laughter. Slow kisses, lazy Sundays, tangled sheets. All the things I could have had. Was Cyan dead?

James blew me a kiss when I fell to my knees, and backed around the building. The rest of my colors left with him.

Darkness called, and I answered. After all, what was the point if my mate was dead?

"Don't dare fucking die on me!"

My sword clattered to the pavement, and someone ripped at my clothes. Heat seared my flesh; the healing almost hurt worse than the strike.

The blood landed on my tongue, and candied apples flowed down my throat. My hand rose, fingers linked, and War's angry face filled my vision. "My Raven?"

Mon Brouillard. I was in desperate need of hiding in the fog at the moment. Never in my long life had I been so vulnerable. I was a god, dammit. Not a fucking demishit!

Who told that bastard I was a demi-doodah?

"There you are, my Raven. I hear you."

My senses came into play; the pavement had been replaced with the cold tiles of our bathroom floor. The air conditioning kicked on, and my skin prickled.

I licked the wounds closed on his wrist, and the darkness called again.

Sleep, my Raven. You will be judging James. You cannot say no, now. Syra's voice floated through my mind, and I obeyed. Her words flowed around me in a plan while Scot worked on getting me clean and into bed.

"We will kill them, my Raven," Scot said as the water flowed over my head and his fingertips massaged my scalp. "Jer works for James. I feel like Jer sent James to kill you. The demigods want war, and they shall have one."

Raven

Syra removed us from the tableau for three days to work out the particulars before thrusting us into the battle.

When she asked us where we'd like to go, my answer was simple. Woodstock, 1969. three days of partying with free-spirited Humans who were loving the moment before Scot and I were thrust into bleeding and dying.

She agreed, set us up with a little garage apartment, and gave us a Pontiac GTO Judge convertible in starlight black. Only five had come off the line to sell, and the sixth one was all mine.

The car was the only thing I remembered in detail after she pulled us through time and space.

Birth was a memory-stealing bitch.

Syra Las Origine- The Source Of All Things

Raven had done what I'd asked. It cost me my firstborn son, and it cost the majick the Anchor.

My Nicky's ashes rested on the mantel, and the rings he and Scot would have exchanged hung from a black ribbon draped around it.

Jeremy killed my Nicky, and Scot killed Jer.

I wound it back to the moment Nicky ashed because I couldn't save him after, and dropped Raven and Scot into Omega Plane. There were twenty-one new ones because Jeremy wielded the goddess of Time's blade.

I wrote a new contract to kill James and set the stipulations myself. Hopefully, Scot would never remember what his brother had done to him.

Oh, making Nyx a part of their DNA taught Peace nothing. Chaos was better at peace than the god himself.

Each new Plane contained everyone in The Veil. There were now twenty-one James' to kill and twenty-one Jeremys to fuck things up. I stipulated seven ticks, and each death would ripple through three Planes.

I also stipulated Raven and Scot would have mates of their choosing and ones Jeremy hadn't touched. Ones strong enough to refuse the damn man. Oh, I hadn't added Nyx's price for participation. Raven and Scot would have children. Sonny was the perfect choice. She had no problems with the situation.

For calling Justice an Amans, the Order word for whore, Jeremy would become what he thought the word meant. I was done playing with them. They unleashed James, taught him the spells to bind and unbind Souls, and the man wore other people's Skins like suits. Half the time, he didn't remove the previous occupants.

Catori, the little Soul Maker who taught him things he shouldn't know, was in for a rude awakening.

Gi was only the beginning of the problem, and she would soon find herself judged.

June 3, 2016- Omega Plane

R aven
My first intake of breath made me smile. A clean woodsy scent filled my lungs under the din of freshly brewed coffee. A roll of parchment landed on my chest, and I snagged it before it bounced to the floor.

My darling,

We are on take two. Please do not ask what happened in tick one. Suffice it to say, my firstborn is dead. There are now twenty-one Planes for James to play in, and he has Twenty-one Vessels to do it in. You are on the Omega Plane, and each death will count three times. I've stipulated seven, but who knows what that tiny tart of a Time goddess will do. She must go when this is over, my Raven.

Save Jaxon from James, and straighten out the money situation. James has turned the Elementals into love slaves. For some reason, the mangy Bear also wants to remove Animals from existence. When James is dead, you will move on to the next Plane.

Syra

I scrubbed a hand over my face and reread the letter, finding her thumbprint in the corner.

I played the memory of Jeremy killing Nick and then ashing the Vessel. Well, hell. I couldn't fix that. The Anchor only got one Vessel until another was born. There was something else she was trying to hide, and I played it all again.

"NICK IS MINE!" Scot roared, and even the memory jarred my teeth.

There was the flash of a mating contract and Syra sobbing about a wedding day.

Well, fuck.

Scot breezed into the room with two cups of coffee and stopped short; his stormy gray gaze glanced at the letter and then met mine. My very logical, unemotional twin had fallen in love and lost him to the demishits.

"I hate them, my Raven."

"I know, Brou."

He eased onto the bed and handed me the second cup of coffee. "Did she say what we were doing?"

I handed him the letter and left the bed to check out our lodgings.

Syra had given us a lakehouse with a private dock and a pool in the front, opposite the lake.

The master bedroom, kitchen, and living room were on the second floor. There were several bedrooms on the ground floor, with the door leading to the pool.

The smell of fresh paint and lemons blended with the outdoors, following me from the living area and down the stairs to the front porch.

The tires of a black Beamer crunched gravel towards me down the oak corridor, and I waited to see if they were going to the house or the separate garage to my right. Green eyes flashed with mischief as she climbed out and held up a white plastic bag. "One mushroom and green pepper with ham?"

She startled me, but I smiled. "Omelette? Yeah. With bacon, fried potatoes, and biscuits."

"Oh, good." She laughed and closed the car door on her way to me.

Six feet tall, long red hair with gorgeous curls, and she wore jeans, a hoodie, and a pair of red Converse. Her arm slid around my waist when she stopped in front of me and breathed me in. "Good morning. Do you like the house?"

She tilted her chin up, expecting a kiss, so I delivered.

Her name was Sonny Felins, she was an interior designer, and we met one night at a bar ten miles from the mouth of the driveway. This was Naples, according to her head. The landmass was different, but all the major cities were there.

Naples was Summer's End, and Summer's Rise was Orlando. Instead of a grand hotel, Scot and I owned a block of buildings there just behind Wall Street.

Scot slid his arm around me from behind, and I drew away, breaking the kiss. She kissed him then, and he was stunned.

Only a god could sustain a god, and another little bomb exploding in the back of my mind was that Jeremy's fuck up meant Scot and I had to mark each other. Sonny agreed to help us and had been for two years. In her mind, I'd grown half a foot, my eyes were now a lighter shade of gray instead of blue, and my hair was three feet longer.

Her Raven had worn it blunted to the shoulders.

Omega Plane was at war, and the Elementals were trying to wipe out the Animals. Sonny's father, Ceael, who'd been a really good friend a lifetime ago, was now mated to a brand new brother in the grand scheme. There hadn't been a Claud in the lineup of Fellidehs originally, but there was now. Catori had been replaced by Claud and his twin, Maya.

Jer and his twin Elijah were the next set of siblings, and they ran The Spa in Orlando.

Sonny's mother was a Viper, and in this scenario, dead. James ran The Spa, and he, along with his men, raided the house one night to steal Ceael. James liked his men pretty- that was, the Skins he wore like suits. James was pasty pale, with rheumy brown eyes and mousy brown hair. No one gave him the time of day if he wore himself.

Her mom died in the fight, and Sonny ran away, ending up in that little bar.

Sonny's Tiger and Viper had come to an agreement, and they worked together, but there was no fur or scales.

Just like our first meeting, Scot was fascinated with her. He thoroughly examined her teeth, tongue, and tonsils before leading her into the house. My twin was stunned. *She's a girl, my Raven!*

I laughed into my coffee cup and followed behind them. Sonny took us to the back deck, and I stopped in the kitchen to make her a cup of coffee, top off my own, and then joined them at the patio table.

She had known the night before and decided to begin with us like she'd started the first time. Instead of buying us a beer, she bought us breakfast.

I eased into a seat, and another Viper walked up the steps and sat down. His dark brown hair winged away from his face like a cobra's hood, and ended in a braid he'd pulled over one shoulder. Sonny set a container in front of him and called him Uncle Liz. He thanked her and raised his eyebrows at me. *Where are we?*

Omega Plane, I thought.

11

Ah. Liz tucked into this food. *Why?*

Jeremy killed Nick Felins, I responded, and Liz paused, his fork halfway to his mouth.

The Anchor to the Planes? The one who kept the world turning for Humans and the stupid Order on one Plane? The one who made sure there was just The Garden, The Shallows, and The Veil?

Yeah, well, The Shallows split, I grumbled.

Fuck. Liz kept eating to keep Sonny from knowing we were discussing things.

The colors filled in information for me. Liz was Lysander Lance, one of the Vipers Gaia thought would make good men. He'd worked for Scot and me in the past, before birth, and Tick one, which Syra didn't want us to remember. The man was my eyes, ears, and informant on the demishits and the other gods. He had worked for Gi, the goddess of Time, in the beginning.

"Are you all caught up?" Sonny smiled around the table, and I arched a brow. "What? This is a brand new Plane, and you need help. You saved me, Raven. I was Order, and now I'm more than that."

"I see." I leaned back in my chair, and she stuck her tongue out at me, causing Scot to laugh.

Okay, I liked her. Just wasn't sure what to do with her.

Sonny

Raven, Scot, and Uncle Liz took the boat out on the lake to discuss the new set of objectives. Oh, I'd heard them talking in their heads. The colors relayed everything to me. The colors I didn't have before James tried to kill me.

I couldn't sustain Raven, but for all intents and purposes, we were married now, thanks to Syra. There was rearranging to do and six demi-doodahs to replace. Nyx was a full doodah for demanding Raven and Scot have children. It was the price Peace set for donating his blood to the DNA cocktail to create Vessels strong enough to sustain Justice and War.

That man would fuck everything up at least three times before he finally got the message. Gi had done something nasty, and James was just a pawn. James still had to die, but Gi also had to be replaced, and I wanted the job.

When Syra asked me who I trusted to help Gemini, I chose Uncle Liz because the man knew all of Gi's secrets, was trustworthy, loyal, and could fight. Jeremy would do something worse than killing Nick, and Gemini didn't give third chances. When it came down to it, Uncle Liz would be the perfect replacement for Jer's majick.

I'd gone to get my clothes from the garage apartment, while the men talked without me.

It was a setup, even the story I gave Raven when we met this morning. Syra had given me memories- dreams, really- and Raven plucked those from my head.

My husband was bisexual and as picky about his lovers as he was about his cars. I smiled at the Black Dodge Charger in the garage bay to my right on my way out the door. Scot's was white. Everything down to color preferences had been carefully planned out, including Raven's male lover.

Nicky was not Syra's only child, just the oldest, and the only demigod. He, like me, held a hint of reptile. His was Dragon to my Viper. Too many bloodlines and DNA choices, and the weaknesses outweighed the strengths as far as the majick was concerned.

My cell vibrated in my back pocket when I made it to the closet in the master bedroom. I pulled it out and one Cyan FeLiSe- all consonants capital. It distinguished gods and demis. His full last name, Felins-Las Origine, was a mouthful, and Syra shortened it to FeLiSe- watched me from the screen.

"Hey, cher. Are they here yet?"

"They are on the boat talking to Uncle Liz right now, Cy."

"What's the plan then?"

"Meet the Menagerie, fix their accounting, snag Jaxon, and kill James. I don't have details yet."

Cy wrinkled his nose over Jaxon. My cousin had been in love with Raven since the man joined him in a fight with James' Vampires. Ones made from Order were nasty and had to be killed a specific way. James bled Cy to get the Sword of Justice. That was a different fight and one I didn't have details for.

Free Will conquered several things, including mating contracts. Free Will included love, and my cousin had dedicated himself to Justice of Gemini.

"I want to see him, cher." Cy sighed.

"Oi!" Azure yelled from somewhere, and Cy smiled.

"I gotta go. We're in town. The fight will be here, so Az and I are staying close. Call me if you need help, and we'll come." The call ended, and I laughed softly. Azure, Cyan's twin, was Syra's Assassin, and Cyan was Ether. If any men in all the Planes could win the hearts of Justice and War, it was the Blues.

Raven

Supper was interesting.

Liz had gone to see if his wife was still his wife when Sonny told him where the woman was. Scot and I grilled steaks and tried to devise a scenario that would work best for feeding. The shakes had started, and the colors were plotting a mutiny.

Without the snarky little shits, we were blind, deaf, and dead.

Sonny, however, initiated the whole thing, and only after did I think about condoms. She still possessed one heartbeat by four in the morning, and I headed down for a swim.

The pool spanned the whole front of the two-story Grand Greek Revival. Altogether there were over thirty bedrooms. Just who was supposed to live here?

I reached the end, and Scot dove in beside me. *I think Jer's men, my Raven. We aren't just saving Jaxon. James has trapped Animal and Elemental alike, and I believe we need to save them all and set them up to live free.*

Why together? Wouldn't they want their own homes? Animals, yeah. We live in Prides, clans, herds... Elementals don't like multi-generational households. Then again, if it's all they know?

Then they can't function alone, Scot thought. *Can we talk about Sonny?*

Okay?

I like her. She also knows more than she's saying, and I can't pull it from her head.

Brou, do you miss Nick?

I'm going to kill Jeremy, my Raven. Just once. If it resets the tick, so be it, but he will die.

Could you wait a tick? I don't remember the first one, but it was brutal, and I sort of wanted a vacation.

Of course, my Raven.

Thank you, Brou.

You are very welcome.

A hand reached into the water before we rolled, and I rose, finding Sonny smiling down at me. "Honey, I made breakfast. There's a Jaxon D'Aubigne on the work phone. He works for Jeremy."

I spotted the cell phone in the pocket of her short satin robe. *Is he in your pocket?*

She wrinkled her nose. *Eww. Yes, he is.*

Before taking the phone, I hopped out of the water and dried my hands on the towel I'd left on the chaise. "This is Raven."

"I apologize for disturbing your morning. I intended to leave a message." Jaxon's voice was gravelly, as if his throat had been ripped out and hadn't healed properly.

"It's not a problem. What can I do for you, Monsieur D'Aubigne?"

Laughter filtered through the phone speaker. "First, thank you for pronouncing my name correctly. Your wife did as well. I don't know how many times I've been called Dawbigknee."

"You're welcome."

Jaxon cleared his throat. "I work for Jeremy Fellideh, who runs The Spa, and am trying to track down some money. We replaced our accountant. Well, me. Jer hired someone to replace me as the accountant, and yesterday he came to me because the deposits he'd personally made after the last party weren't in the account he put them in. There is the deposit, and then five hours later, a transfer."

"And you can't trace the second account," I said as Scot opened the door. I shivered on my way up the stairs from the temperature difference.

"No. Normally, I can, but I've never seen this," Jaxon said.

"Okay, well, we are four hours away at the moment. I can be there by noon?" I suggested.

"Well, I'm actually at Marge's Bed and Breakfast in town? If we could meet for coffee?"

I frowned at Sonny, then.

Naples is a town here. Population seven-thousand. It needs a hotel, pub, coffeehouse? Maybe? It is a stop on the way to the Keys? Sonny raised her eyebrows, and Scot moved to the fridge.

"Raven?" Jaxon said softly.

"I'll text you directions, Jaxon. Come for breakfast. We'll see what you need and go from there?" I said.

"I'll be there. Thank you." The call ended, and I cocked my head to the side.

"I feel like he's expecting something from me," I murmured.

"Oh, well, Gi told him you were his mate. She and Gaia sort of made him dream about you. James tried to kill him behind Studio 54 in seventy-six, and that's the first time Gaia gave him your face and your blood. They hope you'll leave Nick alone if they give you Jaxon." She turned and hugged Scot then, as I caught the egg carton before he dropped it.

"Nick's alive?" Scot whispered.

"No, honey. Your Nicky, my cousin? Very dead. Can't come back from that. This one is Jer's Mon beau, and somewhere around twenty. Connor is his father, but Syra isn't his mother." She rubbed his back, and I took over cooking.

"Someone text Jaxon the address," I said. I also had feelings about the whole thing and kept them to myself.

Had I been so bad that Nick had refused me? Had I gone after Nick? Did I try to steal him in some way?

"No, my Raven." Scot kissed my cheek. "Jer and our parents couldn't tell us apart. They blamed you when it was me, and I didn't steal Nick."

"Okay." The explanation didn't help, but I could do nothing about it now.

"He'll be here in about ten minutes. I told him to come to the back deck," Sonny said.

"Thanks. Um, is Jaxon a god?" I asked.

"I'm not sure," Sonny replied. "I know they were trying to fix him."

Fix. Him. Well, damn. What in the hell had I done in that first tick?

Raven

We'd just sat down to eat when Jaxon walked around the side of the house, dressed in black jeans, a band tee, green Adidas, and carrying a backpack. His brown hair was liberally streaked with ice blonde and fell to his elbows.

Well, goodnight.

He lifted his Aviators and smiled, looking from me to Scot, and stopped. Those warm brown eyes smoldered. *Ah. Here we go again.*

I picked up my plate and stood. "I'll just leave you to it."

Sonny followed me in, and I dumped my food in the trash before cleaning the kitchen.

"Honey, please talk to me?" she whispered, bouncing around behind me, trying to get me to stay still.

I laughed and shook my head. "We are identical, you know. From one look, though, they discard me like a paper towel and-"

She hugged me, then. "He doesn't know you feel that way."

"Scot? No. He thinks I'm asexual."

She jerked her head back and snorted. "He was there last night, right?"

"He's always there. Every time."

"Hmm." She grinned wickedly. "We have to fix that, honey."

"You know I like men?" I asked, and she nodded.

"Not your brother. You aren't wired like that. Some Order don't care," she shuddered, and I laughed. "Did you know there's an apartment in the garage?"

"Is there, really?" I trailed my lips across her jaw.

"There is. And, there's this hot set of twins who-"

I kissed her then because Scot and Jaxon were coming into the house. The colors had given me a play-by-play of their conversation, and Jaxon had asked Scot out. Scot said yes.

Scot and Jaxon settled onto the sofa while I cleared their mess from the patio table.

"He's quite the little woman, isn't he?" Jaxon laughed.

Scot didn't defend me, and I tamped down the urge to take Jaxon's head.

I finished the kitchen and headed to the master bedroom, finding Sonny in a standoff with Nyx, the god of Peace.

"Hello, son." The man smiled, and my colors bristled.

"Sir." Dear gods, I had to bow down to him? No matter how hard I tried, I couldn't like him right now.

"Did Raven meet Jaxon?" Nyx asked.

Sonny kept her face straight and walked into the bathroom, closing the door. "He did, sir."

"Good." Nyx nodded.

"They are in the living room if you want to talk to them."

"I see."

I started towards the closet when Nyx wrapped a hand around my neck and dragged me back down the hall. He shoved me to the sofa beside Scot and glared at us. I flicked my fingers subtly, and Jaxon stilled.

Whatever Nyx was about to dump on us wouldn't be good, and Jaxon didn't need to hear it.

"Why is there a female in your bedroom?" Nyx asked.

"It seems here, I have a wife," I said.

"Ah." Nyx nodded. "Gi did say she'd given you someone for pretenses. Same-sex relationships aren't allowed, so a cover is good. Now. I need you to help Jeremy. He needs funds for a bar, and I expect you to set him up." The man began to pace, and I exchanged a look with Scot. "James knows what he's doing, and has straightened out things here, so leave that part alone." He turned then and arched a brow. "Jer has a mate, Raven, and you'll leave the man alone. Jaxon was made for you."

"What about Scot?" Scot asked.

"Raven," Nyx sighed. "Scot has never been a problem. Even now, he has a wife to adhere to James' laws." He looked around. "This is a nice house. How many bedrooms? Jer would like it here. I'll send him this way, then."

The man disappeared, and Sonny became visible in the hall. She stepped into view, her mouth open in shock. "Just who does he think he is?"

"The Source," I muttered.

Scot snapped his fingers in Jaxon's face, but the man remained still. "Okay, so why does he think Jaxon could sustain us?"

"Syra said Nyx was an ass," Sonny said, oblivious to Scot and me wondering how she was immune to me stopping time in the room. "There's an apartment in the garage. If the grand Doodah sends his precious demi-doodah here, then we are moving there. Scot, you carry on with whatever Jaxon is, and Raven and I will see you later."

Scot's mouth fell open, and he tried to pull me back down when I moved. "You are not leaving me with him!"

"You're Raven remember? I don't count." I jerked away and followed Sonny down the hall.

"My Raven!" he hollered, and I released Jaxon, who continued talking as if he hadn't been paused.

Sonny was already sending our clothes to the garage apartment, carefully leaving Scot's.

Please tell me I have assets here? Me personally? Been making money since it was invented. Dunno what Gi thinks she set up here.

Sonny touched her forehead to mine. *Yes, you have money. A small portion of your assets is in an account.*

"How small? boing, or-"

She laughed and shook her head. "No, honey. None of your checks will bounce."

I loved her at that moment. I tended to say strange things, some reference to an old movie or a book, and people looked at me like I was crazy. Most of the time, I didn't talk and kept my comments to myself.

Then again, she'd had my blood. Well, that was depressing. I made her understand me.

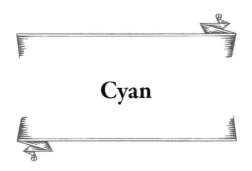

Cyan

Az had been stabbed in the back of the diner. Gi had her own goons and was determined to remove anyone who didn't fit her narrative. I counted spaces with Az to Sonny's colors and found her in a tiny apartment, which didn't make sense.

Mom set her up with Raven and Scot in a grand house.

I jerked the blade out of Az's side, and he bit down on my throat. His scent permeated the air, and Raven skidded into the bedroom. Raven, who I wasn't supposed to see and desperately wanted to. He'd defended me once, a long time ago, and we'd had dinner after. Hadn't seen him since.

The man didn't stop to ask who we were; he immediately began tugging on Az's clothes and patting us both down.

"Oh! Az!" Sonny whispered when she walked out of another door. "We have two bedrooms. Raven, these are my cousins. Syra's sons? Az is her Assassin, and he and Cy share colors."

Azure's head fell back, and Raven lifted him up. "He'd rather be clean, honey."

Sonny nodded and showed us to another bedroom off the tiny hallway. "There's a bathroom in here. You and Cy help him, and I'll bring some clothes."

Raven had done this before, and it didn't take long to strip my twin down and get him in the shower. Raven told me what to do, and I followed directions. In less than thirty minutes, my brother was clean, dressed in shorts, and settled in bed.

"You two just stay here until we leave the Plane?" Raven suggested.

I nodded because I didn't know what to say. He didn't remember me.

Birth sucked.

I followed, in awe of the sealed black glass wall protecting the living space from the three garage bays. There was one door on the left side of the hall beyond the guest room and two doors on the opposite wall. One was open, and "Joey" by Concrete Blonde sounded all over the apartment. Raven walked out singing. He turned and sang to me on his way towards the glass wall.

I found him in the kitchen, to the right of the end of the hall. To the left was a small living room with one charcoal gray loveseat and two modern white highbacked chairs. Surrounding the TV mounted on the wall were gaming systems and controllers under the corresponding units. A white shag rug separated it all, containing the seating in the square.

The next song was Country, and Raven danced as he sang, moving from the fridge to the stove. He raised his eyebrows at me, pointing to the carton of eggs. I smiled; he took it as yes and continued to cook, jamming to the music.

I found the barstools on the other side of the kitchen bar and sat down, watching him. He set a cup of coffee in front of me, along with three kinds of creamer and a sugar substitute. I chose the salted caramel, and he then set a plate of eggs and toast in front of me.

Sonny breezed in, playing an air guitar, and Raven pressed his back to hers as he sang. She laughed; he grinned, turned, and twirled her around.

She handed him a cell phone, and he read the screen, sending a response, and I ate. He ate, too, but didn't get still.

He reached for my empty plate and loaded the dishwasher.

The glass door behind me opened, and Scot walked in, holding hands with Jaxass. The man watched Raven as if he hadn't seen him before, and I could almost see the little rat on the wheel in his head pull the chain for the light. It just dawned on him that he'd chosen the wrong twin. I finished my coffee and walked around to put it in the dishwasher. Raven pulled me into his line dance. I laughed, and he grinned, ignoring Jaxon and Scot.

He pulled my back against this chest, and we rocked as Raven asked Scot what was happening.

Scot watched me and winked before he answered. "We're heading back to Orlando. Jaxon was telling me about a bar he was interested in, and I haven't been to Orlando."

Raven started dancing again. "Cool, Brou. Y'all have fun."

He twirled me around and sang the chorus of "The Tide Is High" by Atomic Kitten to me. Sonny laughed as she joined us, ending up between us, and pressed his forehead to hers after kissing my cheek.

Raven had dismissed them and wasn't paying attention when they left through the man door leading outside. There was a message in there, and Jaxon didn't know what it was.

I didn't expect anything. Raven was himself, and from where I was standing, he was straight.

When Az finally joined us, Raven had opened a garage bay door, moved the SUV outside, and found a grill.

It was a lazy afternoon while Raven stayed busy, and I watched unless he asked me to help him. The man didn't talk. Not out loud, at least. It was facial expressions and music.

Lunch was sandwiches, and supper was ribs on the grill.

Sonny was in and out, and Raven didn't seem to mind that I just couldn't leave him alone. Raven found a patio table somewhere and placed it in front of the SUV. I helped him with the chairs.Az got up in time for supper.

Sonny had given Az something else to wear, and we were just sitting down to eat when Uncle Liz arrived. He kissed Az and me on top of the head, and Raven turned the music down. We could still hear it, but we could have a conversation.

"Rave, man, this place is all kinds of fucked up," Liz said as Sonny brought a bucket of beers to the table and sat down.

"Yeah, Nyx came this morning, telling me Scot was the good son, and I was the pain in the ass. Said Gi fixed the Plane and not to stop James from doing the right thing." Raven rolled his eyes. "The right thing? Then the ass decided Jer should have my house."

Liz laughed. "Oh, Gi set everything up all right. You can't be gay, you can't be Animal, and all Elementals are whores. Syra sent Katarine back to The Veil for me. Gi had decided my wife was James' Amans."

"Did she have to, with James?" I blurted.

"No," Liz shook his head. "I showed up right before his visit. Found her in the bathroom, ready to stab whoever came through the door. Thanks for letting me do that."

"Nah, man," Raven said. "It's your wife. Dunno what Gi is playin' at, but that's not cool."

"I did learn that Jer has THE Menagerie here. His men are the most feared," Liz said.

"Menageries? I outlawed those," Raven frowned. "People aren't chattel."

"Gi has also made everyone think James is Justice," Liz murmured.

Raven burst out laughing. "Why?"

"According to my intel, he has your sword."

Raven arched a brow and held out his left hand. The broadsword landed in it. "Yeah, don't think so." He kissed the shaft, and like Azzy's athame, it slithered down his arm, creating a colorful tattoo of a jewel-encrusted hilt. "Mother fucker wants it now; he'll get me." Raven grinned, and Liz laughed.

"How did he get it in the first place?" Liz asked. "Doesn't that require your blood?"

"If it's like mine, Uncle, it can be wielded by Raven's mate. I know that ain't James, so," Az shrugged.

I slid lower in the seat, and Sonny winked at me. Raven's gaze met mine, and heat rushed from the pit of my stomach to the roots of my hair.

Raven took a swallow of his beer, and then he winked at me. Well, the secret was out now. Just how did Raven feel about me?

Raven

It was midnight, and I was spread out on the roof line of the garage, enjoying the quiet. Cy and Az had gone to sleep; I'd been with Sonny again, just to see what it was like by myself. Forgot the condoms, and now there were two heartbeats in my bed instead of one. One Shiloh Raiden was full of colors and questions, all demanding answers.

It was too soon for all the things I wanted to do with Cy. I had questions, too, and looked forward to discovering the answers. What did he taste like? What was his favorite color? His favorite meal? Did he read? Like old movies?

I wanted the time to savor him but Time had other ideas.

Tires on gravel had my senses attuned to the oak corridor, one fancy red Beamer leading the way. I'd moved Sonny's behind the SUV, leaving the house drive for Nyx's precious Jer. The second was an Audi, and Scot climbed out of the first car while Jer and his twin, Elijah, climbed out of the second.

Jaxon had driven the Beamer and was looking at the closed and locked garage door.

Hello, my Raven, Scot thought.

Hey, Brou. You brought the sheep.

Nyx ordered us here.

Lovely. I didn't move as several beaters pulled in and parked, some cars holding more than four occupants and weren't big enough for two. That had to have been a rough four hours.

Scot led them all into the house, and from the colors, I understood that the men were happy the house didn't smell like sex.

"Somebody find my brother!" Jer ordered. "We want a new bar here, and he's the man to help us!"

Oh, *now*, I was his brother? When he needed money. The colors relayed a conversation from before and one I was sure Syra didn't want me to remember.

Nyx glared at me and shook his head. "Raven. You really have to stop lying. You went to the movies last night with Jer's boyfriend."

"Wasn't me, Sir."

Nyx sighed, stepped back, and put his hands on his hips. "Well. Since you won't leave your brother's lovers alone," he glanced back at Jer. What other lovers? Couldn't they smell? I was a virgin, dammit! Nyx kept talking, though. *"I've had Catori arrange your mating to a suitable female. Her name is Elisabet Felins, and you'll give me grandchildren."*

Lil? They wanted to stick me with Lil? She was fourteen! Got all dopey-eyed when she came in for coffee. Cute, but had that Head of the Council smell. I'd rather be a eunuch, and I'd do it myself before mating to her.

"Has Catori signed the contract?" I asked. Catori was using her majick to bind souls to each other instead of binding them to vessels in the womb.

"Not yet. We are still in negotiations with Elisabet's father," Nyx answered. *"You're Order, so anyone will do, really. I want specific bloodlines, Raven, and he is willing to overlook your deformities. We are paying a hefty groom's price to make this happen, and you'll stop chasing after Jer's lovers."*

Huh. *"What about Scot?"*

Jer snorted. "Scot's normal. He's War, and you're just the spare who refuses to do right."

I ignored Jer. He was baiting me, and I didn't need another reason to piss Nyx off.

"You'll mate to Elisabet, Raven. She'll bear fine young Elementals, who will obey better than you."

Elementals? Nyx obviously didn't understand genetics. I was three different kinds of Feline; my blood would dictate DNA. The Essence could choose their names, eye color, and gender, but the Animal was non-negotiable. Crewe, Gaia's mate, had known that. Why couldn't he have raised us?

"Counter proposal?" I didn't want a wife. Especially not a child. Elementals didn't care, though. They'd sell anyone for the right price.

Nyx folded his arms over his chest, and his jaw ticked. "What would that be?"

"I'll go away." I held my hands up when Nyx started to protest. "I'll go to Summer's End. You can stay here, Jer, date Nick, and if I'm not here, then you can't blame me for anything."

"What about Elisabet?" Nyx asked.

"She's too young."

"Then we'll wait until she's eighteen. I'll just move up your legal age to twenty-five," Nyx nodded. "I'm sure James wouldn't mind."

"James? Head of The Veil Council?"

"Yeah," Jer shoved me. "He's Justice and not a pretender like you."

"Pretender. Scot's not a pretender, then." I took a deep breath and pasted what I hoped was a pleasant smile on my face. "I'm leaving. My assets are mine, and I am going South. I can perform my duties from anywhere, really. Doesn't have to be here."

Jer snorted. "What duties? You chase ass, drink, and are everywhere I go. If I didn't know better, brother, I'd think you wanted to fuck me."

"If I didn't know better, I'd think you wanted to fuck me."

Jer threw the first punch, and we traded blows while Nyx tried to separate us.

"Raven, you are grounded! Stop taunting your brother and do what you are told!"

The lockdown slammed the door on my majick, and my ribs snapped under the next blow; Nyx dragged me off of Jer. Well, I'd gotten in some good licks, too. One whole side of his face was purple.

"Raven, we wouldn't be so upset with you if you hadn't been born. There was only one of you, and Gaia only has twins or trips." Nyx sighed, and I caught sight of Scot peering around the door. "I should have killed you when you were born. Then we wouldn't have this problem. Do you know how shameful it is for three gods to produce an Order child?"

SHAMEFUL. NYX WAS ASHAMED of me. I'd inadvertently given myself the wife; this time, I started in the South. Was I too stupid to do the right things? Had I always been an ass?

Cy landed by my head, and I watched him upside down. *You've never been an ass.*

How did you end up being able to wield my sword? That question still hadn't been answered.

Cy smiled softly and watched the men trying and failing to enter the garage. *You came to help me one afternoon. I had Azzy's Athame long enough for him to take a test at Bridgon's. Mom insisted we have degrees in case we ended up in the world with no way home, ever. Said to always have-*

A backup plan and an out, I smiled.

He nodded. *Well, the first time ever, the Athame snatched me to an alley, and I freaked. You came, we killed some Vampires trying to eat a Human, rewrote her memories, and my majick was tapped. Couldn't get home for a while. You stayed with me, bought me lunch from a hotdog vendor, we went to the movies, and then you bought me supper.*

Sounds like a nice time, I thought.

It was. I was in your city, and you showed me around. When my majick returned, I went home with two things. He held up his wrist, and there was a black thread bracelet with my name.

"BROTHER!" Jer yelled, loud enough to wake Sonny and Shiloh, who'd just settled down. The man stood in the middle of the grass between the house and the garage, throwing rocks at the cedar siding.

I sighed and sat up before I could find out what the second thing Cy spoke of was. "What?"

Jer backed away and looked up. "Oh, hey," he laughed, a nervous little sound.

Cy had shielded himself beside me because he didn't want to meet Jer.

I stood on the 'A' and hopped down, landing on the balls of my feet, noting Jaxon standing on the second-floor balcony of the house, watching.

Jer in this Plane was auburn-haired with brown eyes. Huh, well, there were twenty-one of him, too.

"It's late, Jer," I said, putting my hands on my hips. "Can't we discuss whatever after I've had my breakfast? Say, around nine?"

The door opened behind me, and Sonny walked out in my tee shirt and a pair of my joggers. "Honey? Come back to bed?"

Jer raised his eyebrows at her, and I felt Az and Liz coming out of the garage. The hum of the Athame rolled through the colors. Jer backed away then. "Yeah. We can wait. Nine? Nine is good."

I didn't move until he was in the house, and then I scooped Sonny up. "I have the strangest craving for strawberry ice cream, honey."

"We have that," I said, carrying her to the kitchen.

"With chocolate syrup," she added.

I set her on a barstool, and Cy became visible beside her. He scented her and smiled at me.

Liz and Az walked in, closed the door, and then it walled over, along with the garage bay doors. I needed about five minutes to think. "Why was he afraid of Az?"

"James told them they were Vampires, Rave. Az is The Assassin. He's like their bogeyman."

"I see." I concentrated on scooping ice cream into a bowl. I had several flavors I preferred, and currently, it was strawberry.

"Do we have nuts? I want walnuts," Sonny muttered to herself, and Cy hopped up to see. "Oh, dear gods!"

"Congrats," Az said as Cy sprinkled walnuts onto the chocolate syrup. I set the bowl in front of her, and she sighed.

"It's a boy, honey," I said. "Shiloh Raiden."

"He's talking to you?" Her whole face brightened over that.

"He is. Eat up, now. We'll have pot roast for supper," I said.

"Waffles for breakfast?" she asked, spoon halfway to her mouth.

"Waffles for breakfast." I nodded.

Syra had fully stocked this kitchen, like the one in the house. The one Jer was even now discussing his plans for their future. The ass hat was eating my food.

Raven

At nine, I headed across the yard, leaving Sonny with Liz. I didn't want Jer or any of his men in my garage. Az flanked me, and Cy held my hand.

Fifty men played soccer on my little beach between the house and the lake.

"Travelin' Band" by Creedence Clearwater Revival blared through the speakers, and Scot sat at the table on the deck.

Good morning, my Raven. He held his coffee out to me. Cy took my travel mug, and I pierced my index finger, dripping my blood into the steaming brew. *Thank you.*

Welcome. What does asshat want?

Oh, they are plotting with the money they currently have. They. He didn't pay the men on the beach, and I gave them some cash from the lockbox Jer and Jaxon haven't found yet.

What does he need me for, then?

Oh, Scot smiled sweetly. *He discovered I was Scot, and you are in charge of the money.*

I burst out laughing and took my coffee back, which was now half full.

You told him.

Oh, no, Scot smiled. *Justice comes with the Source's Assassin. Az didn't kill him. It took them three hours to reason out that James had lied and they weren't dead. In the next Tick, I think James might have a henchman.*

The door to the house opened, and Jer walked out. He got too close to me, and Az's shoved his blade between us. "Keep your happy ass over there."

Scot watched Az with a new fascination, and I knew Jaxon's days were numbered.

The gods were playing with the masters of war, and all their plans were coming apart.

The end was coming sooner than later. It felt like a test run.

I hear you, my Raven.

"Let me see what we're working with, Jer," I said, and he returned to the house, coming back with Jaxon and a man I didn't know, who introduced himself as Terrence.

"I've been downtown here and discovered some run-down buildings with no occupants. I was thinking we could refurbish them and-" Terrence started.

"We need a hotel," Scot interrupted.

I hadn't left, so I didn't know what was beyond the driveway. "How big are the buildings?"

Sonny walked around the building wearing another pair of jogging pants and one of my tee shirts. Liz rolled his eyes as he stood behind her. "Honey, Mister McCleden will meet you down at the diner? He's the real estate agent." She rubbed her belly. "I want a burger?"

I laughed softly, and Scot slid the chair back. *My Raven, take care of her and our son? I'll go talk to McCleden.*

Thanks, Brou. "Terrence?"

Jer was busy thinking Cy would be pissed over the baby, and I wanted to bust Jer's face.

I headed down the stairs with Az bringing up the rear. Cy lifted Sonny up.

"Sonny, what is your last name?" Jer asked.

"Why? You gonna run to daddy and tell him how Raven knocked up the wrong bitch?" she asked, and Cy started walking.

Scot laughed softly. "She's feisty."

"She is." Jer nodded. Scot started down to me, and Jer put his hand on his chest. "Where are you goin'?"

"Raven and I will take care of your business opportunities," Scot answered.

"Don't you want to take Jaxon?" Jer asked.

"He can come, too." Scot shrugged.

Jer lifted his chin, and Jaxon joined us with Terrence. This was ridiculous. *Can't they take a piss without his permission?*

Scot burst out laughing, and I grinned, turning my back on Jer.

"Raven, can we talk?" Jaxon asked when we were out of eyeshot of the deck. If they were smart, they could all hear us everywhere but the garage.

NOTHING BURNS LIKE TIME

Scot walked ahead with Terrence, who didn't want any part of whatever Jaxon wanted.

I stopped, put my hands on my hips, and raised my eyebrows.

"You're my mate," he stated.

"And you refused me yesterday by word and deed. Dunno what James told you, but Free Will outweighs anything else. You said no, I moved on, and my bed is full." I kept going then, and Cy smiled at me from the doorway.

Now, that smile was worth coming home to.

My Raven! Scot yelled, and Jaxon's fist slammed into the back of my head. I stopped, turned around, and Jer had come around the house with all his men. Sonny walked out of the garage with Az, who had his arm around her, and his Athame out.

"Raven," Jer sighed. "Around here? Jaxon has the right to fight you to bed you. If he wins, you renounce anyone else, and you're his."

"Fuck that." I cocked my head to the side and waited. "Well? Hit me."

Jaxon's fist flew again, and that time I grabbed it, bones snapping under my grip. He fell to his knees, and I jerked his head back. The skin tore, and dangled from my fingertips by the hair. The majick swarmed me like fireflies and headed straight to Sonny. It ended up in Shiloh, whose colors giggled in my head.

I tossed the head to the ground and realized Nyx, Chaos, and Gaia had arrived. Gi, as usual, was late, but she landed in front of them glaring.

"I made him perfect!" Gi yelled.

"Bull shit." I tossed the head at her feet. "Your turn."

Phi Plane, Official Tick 2

June 3, 2018
  Raven

I woke up to a wriggling and lifted Shi to the floor so he could go potty. Wait. "Shi?"

I caught him up before he got too far and carried him to the bathroom, noting the ghost of a dead girl in the corner, the stale cigarette smoke in the carpet, and the seventies paneling.

My baby boy was almost a year old, judging by size. I helped him, not wanting his bare feet to touch the floor. Long glossy black curls had fallen from his braid while he slept, and I held them out of the way.

Where in the hell was I now?

A black backpack landed at my feet, and I ran my hand through the loop as I carried him back to the bed. Scot stood at the foot of it then, looking around.

"Oh, Gi planned a lovely existence this time," he grumbled and took the bag, pawing through it, handing me the roll of parchment.

I broke the seal to read it, and Shi put his head on my shoulder. "My darlings, you are on Phi now. You killed Jaxon and pissed Gi off. Go to the address at the bottom of the letter. I've sent a nanny for Shiloh, who just wouldn't stay put. Sonny will meet you there soon. You are programmers, and Jaxon will call you again to fix the accounting. Don't kill him until James is dead.

"You have assets, and I've given you some cash in the backpack. Shiloh was born in The Garden, so don't fret about that. He is immune to the time changes after taking Gi's majick from Jaxon. Azure killed James' Omega Vessel after Gi sent you away. I snagged Sonny, and she's been with me. Love Syra."

Scot took Shiloh, and we stripped the boy down, dressed him from the backpack, and rebraided his hair as he ate a brownie that Syra sent. The flavor of Jane caught my attention when he pushed a pinch to my lips.

"Thank you, little man."

"You are very welcome, Papa. Papa, do I have shoes? I would like shoes." Shiloh raised his little eyebrows, and Scot laughed.

"Yes, little man, there are shoes in here for you." Scot pulled out a pair of red Vans, and Shiloh beamed.

His little tee shirt and jeans were black, which he also liked very much.

Scot pulled out two more pairs of black jeans and checked sizes, handing me the bootcut while changing into the skinny jeans. Our tee shirts were also black. We were stuck with the shoes we had, which weren't so bad. Mine were burgundy Pumas, and his were blue.

We stuffed everything else into the bag, checked the room to see what Gi had left us, and crushed the phones before heading out the door.

Parked in front of room two-oh-two of the Blue Ten Motel was a Pontiac GTO Judge convertible with the top down and a blue-eyed beauty who greeted me with a kiss. *Please say you remember me?*

No, but I'll enjoy the reminder? I raised my eyebrows, and he laughed softly.

He lifted Shiloh up and placed him in the car seat in the back, giving him a pair of dark goggles and a beanie.

"Thank you, Cy. Papa, you sit with me!" Shi demanded, and I climbed into the back while Cy drove.

Shiloh shrieked when the car reached sixty mph and squeezed my fingers. He loved it, and it scared the hell out of him.

It took forty-five minutes to get to our temporary home for this tick, and it was a country house with a wraparound front porch.

"No one would ever think Justice and War would live here," Cy said, and Scot turned to grin at me.

Sonny ran down from the front porch, and Cy stopped the car. She leaned over, kissed my cheek, and kissed Shiloh's face. "You scared me!"

"I'm sorry." Shiloh didn't even try to sound contrite, and his mama arched a brow.

"Well, let's go inside and have some breakfast," Sonny said, and Shiloh unbuckled himself. She took him inside, and Scot followed her, leaving me with Cy.

He turned in his seat and smiled. "Okay, this is Tick Two. We had one date before you agreed to this shit, and I had my very first kiss. You were born, shit went South, and I was in The Garden, so I didn't go through any of that with you. We met again in the real Tick one after asshat Jer killed my brother Nick and split the Planes. Twenty-one of those now, and we started on Omega. Seven turns, this is number two. You killed Jaxon. Shiloh stole the man's majick, and here we are."

"What's my objective? It feels like a video game."

He laughed. "Save Jer, save Jaxon, get the Menagerie to be more independent, and kill James. Which may or may not require you to pretend to mate to Jaxon."

"And you? Where do you fit into this?"

"Oh, now, me? I'm your knight in starlight black." He patted the door. "Okay, I'm not this bold, and I rehearsed all that."

I cocked my head to the side and then hopped out of the car before holding out my hand to him. "Show me around?"

He climbed out and walked around the vehicle to stand in front of me. "Sonny is your wife."

"And?"

He pressed his forehead to mine. "We can't feed."

I scented him really well. "We aren't having sex, either."

"We didn't have time last time. Our first date was supposed to lead to our second. We both like to move slow, so I kissed you first. I can't be father to any of the kids that come from this. According to Mom, there will be."

"Hmm. Syra needs me to have them?" I asked, and he nodded.

His lashes rose, and he lifted his head. "Raven?"

Cy was trying, and he chose me over Scot.

Second, he was all my favorite flavors. Third, he was helping us. Fourth-

Can we stop counting? he asked.

Was it a good reason to take someone to bed? No. I still held out for something that might be unattainable. He pushed his hips into mine, and damn. Kissing. We could kiss, right?

"We have to make this work," I whispered, nipping at his lips. Gods, he tasted like he smelled! The colors were returning the memories of our first meeting and the fact that he could wield my sword, which was still firmly on my forearm. It buzzed with awareness- or maybe that was me.

"You'll have to do something with Jaxon."

I smiled. "It won't be hard."

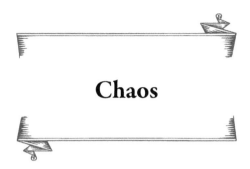

Chaos

T he boys didn't answer when Jaxon called for the accounting app, and Gi brought us to the motel room she'd stuck them in. I'd have to burn my shoes by the time we left. The only occupant was a ghost, who stood in the corner watching Gi peek under beds and look in the drawers beneath the TV.

Gi muttered the entire time, saying, "I put them right here."

"In the drawer?" I asked, and Gaia bit back a laugh.

Gi had lied to us from the beginning, and I'd believed her until Raven ripped Jaxon's head off, and the light winked at me from the ruby in the hilt on Raven's forearm. The boys weren't demigod and Order but gods. Birth hadn't changed them.

"No matter." Gi pulled the hourglass from her skirt pocket, and I stepped forward, wincing as the carpet squelched.

"Cher, what if we wait and see? You've dropped them into a life, and possibly they are out getting breakfast? They do eat." I raised my eyebrows, and Gaia crossed her fingers behind her back. We both wanted Gi to listen and wait.

"All right, but if they haven't talked to Jeremy by the end of the day, I'll set it back. I made Jaxon perfect this time, and Raven just needs to see that."

"Gi?" Gaia cocked her head to the side, "what are we doing all this for?"

"Well," Gi began to pace, "first, we must undo everything Justice has done. The world was just perfect before he interfered." I rolled my eyes and looked to the ceiling as if the answers might fall on my head or Gi's; I wasn't sure which. "Then we have to help Jeremy. He's such a sweet boy, you know. James didn't mean to hurt him. James is just troubled. Bad childhood, but we can't fault him for that." She turned again, and the hourglass fell out of her pocket.

I summoned it before it hit the floor and hoped it hadn't reset anything.

"Gi?" I sighed.

"What? Oh, yes. I have to go," she nodded and disappeared, walking.

"Raven is a good son," Gaia murmured. "Gi and Jeremy got us into this mess."

And Nyx, who was busy trying to find a way into Raven's assets. "We have to find them, cher."

"Raven never has been easy to find. He comes when summoned if he wants to see us. That is really a request, K. The boys don't play by our rules and never have."

"No, we've played by theirs."

"Which started this whole war." Gaia rubbed her temples.

Raven

I bled on the house to shield it, thankful the pool was glassed in. Shiloh and Scot were in the pool when I spotted Chaos and Gaia wandering around the backyard. Sonny started out the door to talk to them, and I pulled her back, kissed her, and told her to stay inside.

My majick covered the stone pavers beneath my bare feet, and I stayed there, waiting for Chaos and Gaia to notice me.

Gaia turned around, frowning, and then her face lit up. "Raven!"

Chaos smiled at me. "Hello, son. Your mother and I were hoping for a conversation."

"Gi is crazy, honey!" Gaia grumbled and took a step forward. She groaned and lifted her left foot. "Stupid woman and her damn motel."

"Where are your shoes?" I asked. They'd always been completely dressed any time I'd seen them.

"The carpet was nasty, son." Chaos lifted Gaia up and carried her to the pavers I stood on. "Gi's convinced Nyx that James is you and that it's your fault James is hurting Jer. So, she made you a boy, which still doesn't make sense."

"Dumb woman thinks that if you die, James and Jer will be perfect." Gaia spit the last word out as if it were dirty. "I'm tired, hungry, and I need shoes!" she wailed, and the rain pelted my skin in fat droplets.

I sighed and let them into the house. "Mom, calm down."

Shiloh counted spaces to me, and Scot hopped out of the water.

Chaos smiled at my son, and Shi hid his face in my neck. "He's beautiful."

"Thanks." I turned and left them with Scot. Shiloh needed to change clothes and take a nap.

Syra had sent me several Toads, who'd worked for me before. Just hadn't seen them since before I was born. They were all around four and a half feet tall, hairless, with wide brown eyes and large blunted teeth.

Gaia had a thing for reptiles and amphibians.

Persimmon met me in the kitchen and held out a towel. I wrapped Shi in it and took the boy to the nursery where Periwinkle waited.

Each Toad's name began with a P, besides Tyrel and Tyrone. I saw Tyrel the most. He was in charge of the rest. Most of them liked to stay shielded, and their shimmers rippled in specific corners of rooms.

Shiloh had gone to sleep by the time he was in pajamas. I laid him on the bed, released my scent, and he pulled his favorite blanket to his nose. Periwinkle sat in the rocking chair, and there were three other Toad-size shimmers in the room, so I left Shi in their care.

I changed before going down to talk to my parents, hoping they'd be gone. According to the colors, they visited on birthdays and left the care and handling of Scot and me to Nyx. Nyx, who loved Jer best.

It scared me to know they'd seen Shiloh. Would they tell Nyx? Would Nyx try to take him away? Would Gi try to kill my baby boy? I didn't trust her not to try to erase his existence.

Cy met me in the closet and eased the tee shirt out of my hand before I tore it apart. "Shh. Gaia and Chaos don't want to be blamed when Gi is punished. The Time goddess will have to be replaced. The woman dropped her hourglass and doesn't know it."

He held that up, and I jerked my head back. "He just gave it to you?"

Cy laughed. "He's afraid he'll accidentally change the Plane before you can kill James."

"Huh."

Sonny hurried in and snatched it out of Cy's hand. She kissed my cheek, and the hourglass disappeared. "Syra has it. It's one of three. So, Gi still has two. Your mother has requested a nap and a pair of shoes when she wakes up. Chaos tells me Gi threatened to change it all if you don't talk to Jeremy before five this afternoon."

"Ah. I need a number, then," I said, and Sonny pulled a cell phone from her back pocket.

"Jeremy had two numbers for you. The second was me." She kissed my cheek. "I sort of added that when Gi was making pretty promises."

"Thank you," I laughed softly and unmuted the call. "This is Raven."

"Hello. I hadn't realized the second number was your wife. I'm Jaxon D'Aubigne. I work for Jeremy Fellideh at The Spa. We need an accounting app."

"Okay, where could we meet to discuss the specs?" I asked, pulling on the black dress pants Cy held out to me.

"The Woods?" Jaxon said softly, and a car door dinged. "It's in Mount Dora."

I looked up at Cy, who nodded and held up ten fingers. "I can be there in fifteen minutes?"

"Make it thirty? Sorry. I'm in Orlando."

"Not a problem. I'll be there."

"Thanks." The call ended, and Sonny took the phone while Cy held up a white button-down.

"Is it a funeral?" I raised my eyebrows, and Cy laughed, producing a black silk one. "Definitely not a date." I snatched a black tee shirt from the hanger, made sure it was the same color as my dress pants, and pulled it over my head.

Cy chose a burgundy pair of Vans, and I winked at him.

My work clothes did not include a colorful noose or a white anything. Cy stood and held up a black suede Blouson jacket, brushing my shoulders off. "I like this."

"Me, too," Sonny nodded.

"Well, change." I looked at Cy. "I'm not going without you."

Sonny leaned around me to see Cy, and I urged her out of the bedroom, meeting Scot on the stairs.

"My Raven, I'll stay here this time. We'll switch after?" Scot raised his eyebrows.

"Keep an eye on Shiloh, Brou," I requested.

"Done," Scot nodded, taking Sonny and kissing her neck. "I'll keep an eye on her, too."

"Let me know shoe sizes, and I'll replace Mom's shoes."

"I will." Scot nodded.

Cyan joined us then, dressed a lot like me, and with Az, who wore jeans instead of dress pants. "Sorry, he's your Guard."

"Where's Liz?" Scot asked.

Az cocked his head to the side. "I dropped him in the kitchen? We were late."

"Ah." I nodded. "Ready to go?"

Cy led us to the garage, and my GTO was in the first bay. On the other side of it was a black Lincoln Navigator, and we decided to take that. Cy played chauffeur, I rode shotgun, and Az rode in the back seat.

I'd established long ago that no one went alone. Order- Animals and Elementals- tended to fight, and one always needed backup in a battle and an escape route.

We pulled into the lot and parked in front of a window to the building. The Woods was an upscale pub full of the Human elite of Mount Dora. Rich older couples who showed up in anything from shorts and sandals to business suits.

The pretty Human hostess greeted us at the door and smiled. "Monsieur Fellideh?"

"That's us, darlin'," Az smiled. She grabbed three menus and led us back to a booth hidden from the dining area, but where the occupants could see everything.

Jaxon had only changed in attitude. He possessed one color in his head, too. Those brown eyes gave me the once over in a slow perusal that had me wanting a shower.

He'd worn a suit for the occasion. Well, it wore him. He stood and offered us a seat. "Forgive my attire. I came from The Spa. If they knew I owned anything fitted, they'd be after my money, too."

Interesting. Why was he telling us that? "You could quit?"

He laughed and chose a different seat when I took his. "I couldn't, no. You know how Menageries work. We're blood bound to Jer and Elijah. Quitting means death, and I like my head right where it is."

Again, Gi had shoved the Order back into Menageries. Why did she think people were chattel?

He produced a laptop and booted it up while the server came to take our orders. When she left the table, he turned the screen for me to see.

There were deposits made throughout the month, large sums of money from particular Order. All high profile. I scrolled through the bank statement, noting that in May, those deposits were being transferred into a different account.

"I can't trace it. I was hoping you could find the account?" Jaxon asked.

It made no sense to me until I got to the last withdrawal, and it stated Groom's Price for Jaxon D'Aubigne to mate to James Felins. I raised my gaze to Jaxon's, who lifted a shaky hand. His fingers massaged his temple.

"I can't," Jaxon whispered. "It won't work."

"What's your aversion to James?" Az asked.

Jaxon's gaze flitted to his and then back to me. "I'm mated to Raven."

The server arrived again, and Az took the laptop, passing it to Cy while she put our plates on the table.

I took a minute to scent the room and, most importantly, Jaxon. The man possessed several sexual scents; the most prominent was Jer. Well, some things never changed. Someone told Jer Jaxon belonged to me, so Jer fucked him.

Jaxon projected his thoughts loudly. His mother had given him my blood, promising I'd fix it all. Jer wanted him to renounce me after. Then Nick showed up, and Jer was all about him.

I was Jaxon's last hope to save him from a mating to James.

I've seen this show, Az thought, and I took a swallow of my beer after the server popped the top off in front of me. She knew who I was, and she was Human.

That they were saving a cheerleader? Cy asked.

Jaxon leaned closer when she left the table. "I can't mate to James. He's Justice. I want a nice guy who doesn't mind what I do on the weekends and always waits for me when I get home. You have a nine-to-five, and you're married, so what's the conflict?"

There were so many answers to that question they made my head spin.

"What's wrong with Justice?" Az asked.

Jaxon snorted. "Have you met James? He's ugly, for one. I could get it up for Raven. Sex once, and then we just need to feed. James wants to share my bed and doesn't want me with anyone else. I have to make a living."

"Do you like your job?" I asked.

Jaxon grinned. "I do, yeah."

Dear gods! Gi wanted me to have someone who-who, I couldn't even say it.

"Jaxon, who is your mom?" Cy asked.

"Gi." He shrugged. "Raven's lower than me since he's Order, and I'm a demigod. He has to prove he can support me."

And there it was. I sat back and watched the man shovel food into his face. He cleaned his plate, and I pushed mine towards him. Jaxon took it as acceptance.

Cy and Az took it like me. Jaxon was crazy, and his words didn't match his feelings or his very evident hunger. He needed someone to financially support him.

I paid the check when Cy held up a USB key.

"Jaxon, we'll be in touch," I said, and he frowned.

"Don't you want to see my house? I have a music collection. You like music. We-"

"I'll be in touch." I arched a brow, and he got quiet.

Az and Cy flanked me on the way out of the building.

"Cy," I said, turning to wait on him, and slipped my hand into his. "I'm starving."

He laughed. "Sure. We'll stop on the way home."

There were so many things wrong with Jaxon I couldn't begin to name them all. He thought I'd actually take him after the things he said.

"That was my fault," Az said from the back seat. "I sorta told him to tell the truth. Then I told him to tell Jer we'd fix the money. Pretty sure with all those scents on him, he's probably a very smooth talker. Nothing in his tiny brain said he'd been forced into anything."

"I can't like him. I'd have to be beaten down pretty far to see him as a way up," I said.

"Raven, made gods don't eat. Gi's slow, so I don't think she understands how she's treating her son," Az murmured. "Especially if she thinks everyone is a commodity."

"Azzy, it also doesn't help that Order pay brides and grooms' prices for matings."

"I changed that." I rubbed my forehead. "I set different stipulations."

"Yeah, well, Gi didn't like the new way, so she wants it all back the way it was," Cy sighed.

Raven

I'd solved the money problem by four-thirty in the afternoon, and sent Jer a message directly, bypassing Jaxon altogether. I even ruled on the mating.

Cy, Shiloh, and I were at the little gas station about five minutes from my house when Jer called me. I was trying to have a small second date before the world burned again.

"The contract burst into flame," Jer said by way of greeting.

"Yes, because I'm Justice, brother. We need to have a little chat. You and Elijah come to the address I'm sending you. Don't bring Jaxon or I'll kill all three of you and we'll start again."

"Done," Jer agreed.

"Seven-thirty." I ended the call and texted him the address.

Cy walked out of the little store with Shiloh, who held up a cup with a black spoon sticking out of it.

"They make ice cream, Papa! She gave me a black spoon when I told her pink was itchy." Shiloh glowed with happiness, and Cy laughed at the boy.

"Cool! What flavor did you get?" I asked, taking him to put him in his car seat.

"Butter pecan," Cy murmured.

"With chocolate syrup," Shi nodded.

"You gonna cover everything in chocolate?" I asked and Shi giggled.

"Not meat, Papa. I don't think I'd like that."

I drove that time, and reached for Cy's hand. "Meeting with Jer and Elijah, put little man to bed, and-"

"I'll be up after you tuck Sonny in, too, Raven." He kissed my knuckles.

"And if I bring Scot?" I asked.

"He can entertain Azzy." Cy arched a brow and I laughed.

49

"We'll do that."

Only, it didn't happen.

Jer showed up early, and brought James.

I made Cy stay in the house, and Scot joined me in the driveway.

The money was fixed, I'd saved Jaxon from James, who was livid that I'd taken his mate away.

Jer and Elijah flanked the man, backing his play. James held out his left hand and frowned when nothing happened.

"Looking for this?" The broad sword slithered down my arm and the hilt filled my palm. "I am Justice, James."

One swing, and James' head hit the gravel with a thud.

The world swirled around me, and Scot grabbed my hand. I had a feeling the next time, Jer wouldn't just be cockblocking.

Sigma Plane Tick One- Again

R aven

The fight that lasted less than two minutes still played on a reel in my head. Would the stench of death ever wash off?

Scot propelled me forward carefully, catching me before I kissed the porch floor and leaned me against the wall.

"My Raven, just be still. We'll be inside in just a second, and you can lie down."

The lizards darting around in the shrubbery caught my attention, and I laughed, causing my side to twinge and breath to catch.

Every little thing would be a permanent reminder of what happened in the dark before dawn. The litany of assurances from the colors began again as they tried to reason with me.

Hah! Reason with. Understanding and comprehension still weren't shaking hands yet, and Scot touched his forehead to mine. "Brou?"

"I love you, my Raven," Scot murmured, kissing my cheek. "Inside. Then I'll get groceries."

"I want a burger," I gritted out when my jaw refused cooperation. "Maybe not."

Scot helped me over the threshold and the step up was jarring.

I froze inside the door when the scent of barbecue slapped me in the face. The night before had been educational on so many levels, and 'barbecue' meant Elemental. 'Flower power funeral parlor' meant Vampire, and it all mixed unpleasantly with my own scent.

Somewhere in the townhouse was a young man, and we weren't expecting company. Scot closed the door softly, and I stayed put as Scot shimmered into fur to hunt.

Scot padded silently through the little hall. I lost sight of him when he rounded the stairs but could still see what Scot saw through those blood-red eyes.

Scot found the young man in a bedroom, and I was off the mark on the Elemental part. The Viper was masking his scent on purpose, and his tongue flicked out to taste the air half a second too late.

He turned and was face to face with Scot.

"Holy damn!" the man whispered and backed into the closet. "Okay, I'm Lysander. You know me; you just don't remember. You're War. Where's Raven?" His tongue flicked out again, and he darted around Scot, unafraid the Cat would eat him. When the man emerged from the shadows, I slid down the wall. "Oh, gods! Rave!" Lysander hissed as the colors checked out completely, and warmth coated my upper lip.

The blood reached my tongue at the same time Scot's pleading did. Someone left us vials in the fridge but we didn't know who, only that we needed it to heal.

Lysander was trying to explain something, but it was in the wrong language. Our Felines spoke French.

"Je ne comprends pas!" Scot yelled, and I opened my eyes again. The blue beneath the surface of my twin's inner wrist called to me with scent and sound. For the second time in less than twenty-four hours, the pressure built in my gums, and I wrapped my fingers around the source of the want. Scot stilled when I bit down, and our eyes met as I linked my fingers with his.

"Good," Lysander murmured. "What idiot told you not to feed?"

"Didn't know we could." I sighed, and Scot stared at his unmarred skin.

"Montre-moi," Scot demanded and touched his forehead to mine. The colors made explanations, and Scot beamed before his fangs descended he and eased them into the flesh beneath my ear.

"You are?" I asked as Scot eased into my lap and sat down, careful not to rip my throat out.

"Lysander Lance, your First, Gemini." The man squatted down in front of us. "Noir sent me as soon as he found you this morning. You have all your assets, and we have the connecting units to this townhouse. Your parents have been looking for you."

"We have those?" I asked as Scot licked the wounds closed and tucked his nose into my neck.

"Yes, Gi is trying to kill you. It's taken a while to find you, and it looks like she rewrote some history, too." Lysander glared at the floor. "Now, there is food. I went to the grocery store after I bought your clothes. I am your man of affairs while we work on killing James in all twenty-one Planes. You'd killed him in several, and Gi started it over. We have four more ticks to go after this."

"I did that last night," I murmured.

"Interesting. You killed James last night?" Lysander frowned and pulled out a cell phone. "This is Delta Plane."

"Hey, can I have one of those?"

"We have them, my Raven," Scot mumbled. "Please say you feel better?"

"I do." I kissed the top of his head. "I'd really like a shower?"

"You do smell better," Scot whispered.

"That's because you are mated, and your scents blend. I didn't recognize you earlier because you still smelled like candied apples," Lysander replied. "the chocolate and caramel were missing."

"Mated?" I frowned, and Lysander laughed as he shook his head before pointing to our positions.

"Gi left a lot out of the retelling, didn't she?"

"Don't tell me," I muttered, and Scot flinched. "Shh. I'm good. Just don't want to discuss that with Scales."

"Okay, my Raven."

"You killed James this morning?" Lysander asked, changing the subject.

"Yes." Scot nodded.

"Did anything around you change?"

"Too busy breathing to notice," I replied. "Shower? Food? My jaw works now."

Scot helped me to the bedroom to shower first.

We'd lived here for twelve years, and the only difference now was the view from the bedroom window. Suddenly, there was another window in another house. We didn't have neighbors before.

James was still alive.

The details were too small to remember when the days were filled with bleeding and dying. Now that Lysander called attention to it, I would make a conscious effort to pay attention. The details were important. After meeting the

53

objectives, the board was reset, and we were shoved into the game again. It all made sense now. So many people gone, and then suddenly they were there again.

The world moved around us, and little things marked differences. The different Planes.

Gods, I couldn't wait for the finish. We weren't nearly done, and I was so very tired.

Theta Plane Tick Four

Jer

I leaned against the paneled wall that had been cinderblock the night before, but Elijah was the only person to notice. James was ranting about the 'little shits' again, and his protests from the previous evening about sending Jaxon in to kill them had changed to "he's your best fighter, and I want them dead."

Men were missing from the meeting, and their chairs were empty. The 'little shits' had killed them in the failed purchase. I wasn't so sure the boys James promised were as agreeable to becoming Menagerie as the man stated. I also wasn't sure James wasn't the purchaser instead of the protector he'd claimed to be.

Jaxon entered the office and took his place beside me on the wall, but he was more reserved than normal. The man's scent had a new variance, and I swallowed bile. James had taken 'punishment' to a new level, and Jaxon was now his whipping boy.

Elijah's eyes met mine before he stood from behind the desk. "Where are they now?"

"Kyle stole them!" James glared at the floor. "We need those boys!"

Now they are boys? I thought. Elijah heard me but didn't respond.

"How old, James?" Elijah asked.

"Sixteen. You have to get them away from the Dragon, or they will be useless to recoup our losses," James said.

Our? When did the losses become his? "Sixteen puts them where? What kind of background are they coming from?"

"They are poor. The promise of food, clothing, and shelter should make them do anything we ask." James nodded, and Jaxon cleared his throat.

"I need a scent," Jaxon murmured, and James arched a brow in his direction. "My lord," Jaxon added begrudgingly.

When James had taken that title?

James tossed a nearly shredded article of clothing onto the desk, and the shield surrounding it fell, releasing the scent of clean cotton.

Jaxon had candles in his room smelling like that, and I understood several things at once. First, the scent belonged to Jaxon's mate; second, James wanted that mate dead; and third? James wanted to break Jaxon's will first. Whether that was a part of the objective or not, it had begun.

Jaxon moved forward and lifted the fabric up, revealing several lies simultaneously. The tee shirt came from the Hollow and, if I wasn't mistaken, cost around two hundred dollars. The blood on the shirt was James', and the amount and spatter pattern indicated a kill.

We weren't after poor boys; we were after seasoned fighters with the money to hide in plain sight, and James was a dead man. We were housing the enemy of someone strong enough to kill the man we'd come to call Enforcer.

Brother, we are after gods, Elijah thought.

Why would two gods be living here? I questioned.

The war is here? Only two I can think of are strong enough to kill James. You know as well as I do that if we were, we'd take his head and be done with the whole mess. That death blow ricocheted across planes.

Gemini, I responded.

Exactly. As far as I know, they've never had Vessels.

Which means they were born and are going through Estrus. Every Order, no matter the gender, went through the heat at sixteen. It stood to reason born gods did, too.

Jer, born means...

Loss of memories, Elijah. I know. James thinks to literally catch them unawares.

Then he doesn't know he died last night.

I'm not so sure that 'he' did. I think there is one of him for each plane.

"Well? Where are they?" James demanded.

"It's a scent." Jaxon arched a brow at him. "I have to leave the building to track it."

"No. No, I don't like that idea at all," James said as he paced.

"I'll go, then," I volunteered. "I do need Jaxon to run some errands for me. We have a party Friday night, and we do need the money. The men won't work for free, James."

"That, he can do." James nodded. Had he been that stupid the night before? No. The Flesh remembers what the Essence forgets, and James lost more than one Vessel and the knowledge that came with the experiences.

"Good. Can we go now?" Elijah asked. "I do have things to accomplish."

"Yes, yes." James waved us away, and Jaxon hid the shirt on our way out. I followed him to his room, and when the door was closed, I urged him into the hidden hall behind the closet. Elijah met us in the dark, and we took Jaxon to the garage.

"Talk," I said while driving through the back gate. Jaxon looked out the window of the backseat and sighed.

"Kingsford Place," he answered.

"That is not what I was asking, and you know it," I grumbled. "What did James do to you?"

"Kingsford Place," Jaxon said again as if it was his military ranking, and he didn't have to give any other information.

"Fine. Which townhouse?" I asked.

"Three-oh-five to three-oh-seven."

Tracking for us also meant memories, and Jaxon pulled the shirt out again, picking an unbloodied spot to scent. The conversation was over as the man's lavender eyes reflected scenes from the night before.

It was too fast to follow from the rearview mirror, so I concentrated on driving.

There was a gate with a keypad for entry when I arrived, and Jaxon told me to pull up far enough so he could put in the passcode.

Well, damn. The man didn't trust me anymore.

We were a part of whatever he remembers, Jer, Elijah thought. We, however, remembered a completely different scenario from the night before, and Jaxon wasn't in it.

The gate swung open, and Jaxon rolled his window up as I pulled through. The man gave me directions to the very back of the complex, and I got my first look at the 'boys' James wanted them to find.

They were standing in the open garage of the center townhouse setting up band equipment.

The walls had been soundproofed, and the six-seven, raven-haired young men were dressed in nothing but black shorts that came to their knees. From the curb, I couldn't tell one from the other as they both turned to look at us at the same time.

Another man emerged from the townhouse carrying two bottles of soda. The poor boys had a servant. The man's job title immediately changed to bodyguard when he entered the drive, and the bay door closed behind him.

I slowly climbed out of the car, aware that Gemini's first line of defense was equal to us.

"What in the hell are you doing here? They don't want to see you, Jer." He sighed and folded his arms over his chest. I was trying to place his very unforgettable face and coming up empty. As far as I knew, I'd never met a man with green-scaled brows and blood-pink eyes. There was no discernible pupil when I looked at him head-on, and the fact that he had brown hair past his elbows was incongruous with the lack of brows.

"You have me at a disadvantage," I stated as Elijah joined me. Jaxon, however, had boldly walked up to the front door and into the townhouse.

"Good gods!" The man pinched the bridge of his nose. "Can't you people just leave them alone?"

Someone shrieked none too happily, and the bay door opened again.

"Liz? Can we have barbecue for supper?" One of the twins requested as he backed away from Jaxon. The other was stalking Jaxon with four sets of sharp-looking fangs and a clawed right hand.

"Scot, don't eat him, now," Liz replied, and Jeremy knew exactly who the fanged man was.

"*My* Raven," War growled, but Jaxon didn't take the strong hint. I hurried into the garage and jerked Jaxon away from the hand poised to gut him.

"Jaxon, they are mated," Elijah said softly. "War is refusing you."

"At least you haven't forgotten them. Realized they aren't Amans yet?" Liz arched a brow, and I sighed. "Jaxon, I'm afraid you are caught in a snare."

Raven jerked Scot to him, and the fear rippled away from them in shuddering waves. They shimmered in and out of view until they were both just gone.

"Why are they afraid?" Jaxon asked.

"What are you doing here?" Liz asked, ignoring the question.

"James wants them dead. He's also slow, and nothing the man says makes sense. Didn't want Jaxon to meet them," Elijah replied.

"So you brought him?" Liz sighed as the door opened leading into the house, and Raven peered around it, slamming it closed when he saw we were still there. Once more, it opened, but another man emerged. "Noir, hey."

"Lysander, the boys are fretting. I see why now. Jeremy, you and Elijah have to leave them alone. They are renegotiating the terms of the contract," Noir stated.

Contract? Ah, hell. We were in the middle of a different war. Chaos and Gaia wanted James dead, and Jaxon was the cheese at the end of the maze.

"What do we tell James?" Elijah asked.

"It's not Gemini's problem. They'd have been more apt to help you if you hadn't called Raven an Amans and interred Scot's mate, Jeremy. Compound that with the attempted rape and murder of their Vessels last night? They meant it when they said they didn't want to see you ever again."

"You reek of James," Lysander stated. "The friend of my enemy?"

"Is dead," Elijah whispered.

"Yes, and they can kill you, too," Noir murmured as the door opened again, and Raven and Scot stepped out of it holding hands.

"Please talk to me," Jaxon pleaded. "I don't know what I've done."

"We'll go," Raven said, ignoring the man, and I frowned.

"We didn't come here to take you," Elijah said.

"He did," Raven replied, and Jaxon flinched. "We can't kill Jaxon. If we do, the tick starts over, and the death doesn't count. Your precious First has betrayed us again."

"Why go?" I asked.

"We can and will kill James anywhere. You think your little army will stop us, but you forget the rules I taught you in the womb, Omega," Scot said, referring to me by my majick. It was my duty to end civilizations. "Tonight, I will take your head, and you will remember."

"Will the deathblow to James count?" Noir asked.

"Yes," Gemini answered, and Jaxon pulled the zip ties from his back pocket. The turn of events shocked me, and Jaxon wasn't happy about it either. James' protests made no sense.

"They do, Omega," Raven laughed, but it sounded bitter. "The bastard expected me to take Jaxon to bed. As if I want your leftovers."

"I've never been with Jaxon," I murmured. Just what had I been doing I couldn't remember?

"Scents don't wash off of the Essence or the flesh. Remember your Sins, Omega. Liz, we want a house," Scot said as Jaxon pulled them toward the car.

"What in the hell is really going on?" Elijah asked Noir. "I don't want to go back if they are going to attempt to kill us. We didn't come to fight."

"Bullshit!" Lysander laughed. "You will die tonight. They got permission; they were denied the first time."

Lysander

I found myself on my back in a study I knew all too well, with a large black Liger touching his nose to mine.

"Lysander, darling. We have a problem." Syra's voice reached me from somewhere to my right, but I was busy staring at a pair of angry amber eyes.

The Liger backed up enough to sit between my legs, and Syra plunged a blade into my heart. The pain was excruciating, and the end of the agony didn't happen for several long minutes.

My limbs were on fire, and my heart beat around the blade that had severed it in two.

"I'm afraid you'll have to go home now, and the boys will fight on without you for the moment," she said as the blade was removed.

Betrayal crawled over my skin and pricked my senses as the majick settled into my Vessel.

"Oh, gods!" I rasped. "What have you done to me?"

"Always have a backup plan, darling. You are mine." Syra smiled, and Shiloh peered at me around her.

"What happened?" Nothing made sense anymore.

"Gi changed the game and has stolen several of my sons."

I hadn't seen Cy and Az in a while, and the Liger watching me was Lucah, if I remembered correctly. "Sons who were strong enough to take on the majick after judgment," I sighed.

"Yes. You now possess Jer's and Elijah's majick, Liz. And you are my son."

"Why me? Why not tell Gemini to-" I answered my own question. She couldn't find Sonny, either, and Sonny was the only female Gemini would touch.

"Gi will have a very hard fall," Shiloh purred, sounding very much like his father.

Alpha Plane

A ugust 1, 2016
   Raven

Someone had fast-forwarded my world and stopped it in a chair. I was still waiting for the colors to catch up as Jer stood beside me, checking on the take from the night before.

My nose started to bleed, which was a normal occurrence these days. The only parentals I saw were Nyx and Gi after Jer rescued Scot and me. That part didn't make sense, but the colors said it happened.

The snarky little shits also told me I was madly in love with one Jaxon D'Aubigne, who was in love with Scot.

Nyx told me to share because no one had thought about me. Gaia, who was supposed to mate people, forgot I needed a mate.

Jer handed me a handkerchief and I took it. The man droned on about something but I was two tired to focus. I'd been up since Friday night when we opened the club, and it was currently Monday morning. Hadn't fed in two weeks because Scot forgot every morning.

I put blood in his coffee and Jaxon would walk in, distract him, and I was forgotten. Almost as if Jaxon was waiting for the moment so I didn't get to feed.

"I want you to see about it tomorrow," Jer said, pulling me back to the conversation.

"No. Tuesday is my day off. In fact, after I deposit the money, I'm done."

Jer jerked his head back and frowned. "Who told you that?"

"Right." I stood, catching myself on the back of the chair. "I quit."

Jer laughed. "No, no. Just go make deposits and here's twenty," he pulled his wallet out and gave me a twenty dollar bill. "Get lunch. You'll feel better after you eat."

That was another thing. Scot had to eat. Scot could eat for us and sleep for us. Feeding, not so much. He couldn't feed for me. Jaxon couldn't sustain us both.

I took the deposits and left the office, heading to the bank. Well, to see Suzie, Keeper of All things Bright And Shiny. I left the money with on her desk, but had never met her in person.

Took me ten minutes to reach the building on foot, and another three to reach Suzie's office. I set the bags on her desk and fell into the chair in front of it.

"Raven?" Hot air blew in my ear, and the smell of sardines followed. I opened my eyes to find a bright blue liberty spike bobbing above my head.

It was attached to a female with no eyebrows or lashes, watching me with round green eyes.

"Um, hey. I'm sorry. Just tired." I started to get up and she moved to stand in front of me.

"I'm Suzie. I've been trying to catch you. Only one of me, and twenty-one Planes." She croaked, and her large lips split into a grin.

Suddenly there were four other people watching me. Two with stormy gray eyes, and two with ice pink.

"Suzie, we'll go to the barn?" the tallest announced.

"Papa can sleep there," the next one said.

"If you're sure? Jer will be looking for him, Shiloh," Suzie replied.

"I'm sure."

And then we were moving, and I had to wait for my stomach to catch up that time.

"Kansas, you and Tris get Papa in the bed. Amy and I will sort the kitchen. TY!" the boy hollered.

"Here we are."

My eyelids were too heavy to follow the conversation and who was speaking.

The bed dipped around me and the scent of green apples and caramel wafted under my nose. Hot blood dripped to my lips, and I licked it away, bringing my hand up and claiming that wrist.

"Drink, ma Leuer. Then you can sleep while I tell you a story." He settled down beside me and his heartbeats set the colors swaying to a happy rhythm. "Once upon a time, there was a beautiful, strong warrior, named Justice."

I licked the wounds closed, and he moved then, brushing his lips across mine. He continued, and I listened.

64

"There was also a young god named Azure, who was taking a test, and left his Assasin's blade with his twin, Cy. They'd done this many times before, but this time, the majick needed Az, and the blade sent Cyan to an alley in Summer's Rise.

"Cy didn't fight back then. He'd never had to. So when the Order Vampires came after him, he prayed for help. Who answers the prayers of gods? You do, ma Leuer.

"You came, and removed their heads for me but you couldn't send me home. I lived in The Garden, you see, and you had vowed to stay out of it. You never lie. I wanted to spend more time with you, and we took a walk. You bought me my first hotdog, took me to my first movie, and then to dinner.

"After, when my majick returned, you kissed me goodnight, and asked me to meet you the following Friday night. I agreed. Then an evil Time goddess had other plans and sent her nasty goon named James after me. James took my blood in another fight, and used your sword against you.

"You were born, and it took three gods to create a Vessel strong enough to sustain you. Birth made you forget, and you ended up with siblings who hated you. Jer is your brother, and he is a pain in the ass. Every single time, he's stopped us from this."

"Where have you been," I whispered.

"Guarding your son, Shiloh. You now have Shiloh, Kansas and Tristan who are twins, and Amy. Gi found out about me and dropped me into the game. Az and I have been pretending to be Jackals, which is hard, since we possess two lion hearts."

"If I claim you now, what happens?"

"We are on the last Plane, ma Leuer. Unless Gi finds out about this barn and your children, we will go home to The Veil when you kill James."

I rolled him over, and stripped his tee shirt off, before tearing at his fly.

His cock twitched, and I scraped my fangs above it, piercing my index finger. A tear drop inked into the flesh, and I took him in my mouth.

Memories flooded my colors, and I contained them to me, so Scot didn't know what I was doing.

Something bad was coming, and I wanted five minutes to savor my mate. The one person who'd come to find me when everyone else left me to drown.

He tensed beneath me, pulsing into my mouth, and I swallowed it all.

I crawled up his body, and laid down again, as he returned the favor. We didn't have time for more.

Tristan and Amy were arguing somewhere below us, and we wanted to establish the bonds, even if it was only halfway."

And then all hell broke loose.

The walls shimmered around me, and the door moved. Gi had done it again.

Alpha Plane Take Two

Kansas
        The damn tick started over and I didn't know why. We'd been careful up to this point. My money was on Suzie.

Shi had vanished, leaving Tristan, Amy, and me. Gi breezed in, announcing Tristan was a D'Aubigne, and that Amy was Jaxon's daughter.

Papa also had another daughter, who I was sure belonged to Scot, but Gi swore Olivia Grace was Jaxon's, too.

I ended up with a Lion named Colt, who was supposed to grow up with Tris and me in some tragic story about a drug addict mom with mean boyfriends. Colt was Cy's younger brother. He wasn't mine, but when Gaia heard about us, she automatically tried to mate us.

I had to claim Tristan to keep them from separating us. We were twins and it didn't matter that he was Scot's son.

Jaxon pretended by day that Papa was the love of his existence and at night, he was trying to corner any of us he thought would be willing, including Tristan and me.

Papa took us to the beach, along with the Blues who were somehow supposed to be Jackals, and Olivia's promised mates. My little sister was two and didn't need mates.

The god parentals were crazy.

Charlie and Armand were next. No one knew where Armand had come from. Charlie was also Cy's and Az's brother. Charlie and Colt were identical aside from their eyes. Charlie's were amber and Colt's were blue.

Entering stage left in the new role of Scot's mate was Christian D'Aubigne, Jaxon's twin. Gi had put both of them together with bubble gum and James' spit.

They were abusive in this play, and Dads were just trying to get to the finish so we could all go home.

Gi stirred the shit pot with a Justin stick, adding Jaxon's first love into the mix. Justin was an ass and only wanted Jaxon back.

Justin swore he was in love with Papa, who didn't want either man.

We were currently in the new house, and Az and Cy were arguing. Az needed to feed, and needed Cy to mark him.

Cy, however, wouldn't touch anyone. I knew why but no one else remembered.

Cy followed Scot around like a puppy but Dad wouldn't give him the time of day. Az hit Cy, and the most extraordinary thing happened. A broadsword with a ruby in the hilt filled Cy's palm.

"Holy hell!" Az backed up as his Athame slid into his hand. "I yield!" Az screamed. "I yield!"

Someone pulled on the puppet strings, and I landed in Syra's study, with Amy and Tristan.

Shiloh, whom I hadn't seen in years. Or was it months? Who the hell knew with Gi? Was standing in the middle of the floor wrenching Gi's head back.

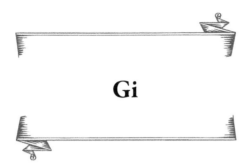

Gi

I'd reset the board so many times before they made it to the end that it was a wonder anyone remembered their names. Someone's will was stronger than my directive, and Jaxon kept dying.

It was supposed to be easy. I'd made Jaxon perfect for Gaia's youngest brats. Those boys had nothing to do but kill James so Catori's mate could take James' place. After birth, there was no Gemini, only the demigods.

Raven just couldn't stop himself and kept killing my Jaxon, but I was done playing with them. Letting it end was the only way to fix it, as I summoned the contract they signed the second time. I ticked off each thing negated and smiled at the final clause. Catori was brilliant. The last line would send the boys straight to The Veil Club, and they would be gone for good.

And the Dead Shall Rise.

Now, the only thing left to do was to make sure Gemini's children died, too. That was Catori's job. Play with the majick, swap a few Essences, and the children had no mates.

I couldn't wait.

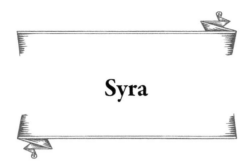

Syra

Raven wrote journals from one Tick to the next, and I'd been reading them during Gi's last play. It was the last and an end to Gi's and Nyx's reign.

The contract on the coffee table shimmered out of view for a moment, and when it returned, all lines but the last one were black. I sat up, flung the journal onto the coffee table, and snatched the contract. Blood had seeped into the parchment, tearing it in two, but I only needed the last line.

Catori would die next. I'd make sure of that. The one who'd killed my sons? Would see me now. In this moment. Camryn, who'd died when Gi tried to make him someone else in the game, and Nicky, who'd been used and abused because of Gi's machinations. Jesse, who'd done nothing to deserve the blade in his back. Blaine, my sweet baby boy, who'd fallen in love with Shiloh Raiden and died for it, just like Nicky had for loving Scot.

"GI!" My roar shook the foundations, and the tiny Time goddess landed in the study holding her second hourglass like a weapon. The third, I had a sneaking suspicion, was in The Veil.

"Oh." Gi stood straighter and glanced around the room, pausing on each face etched into the urns on the mantel. "My Lady."

I snatched the hourglass from the woman's hand and slapped her in the face. The hourglass shimmered out of view, and I picked up the journal, flinging it at Nyx as he filled the doorway from the hall. Chaos, Noir, and Gaia peered over the god of Peace's shoulder.

I curled my lip, nodding towards the book. "Open it. The last entry. Tell me what you see?"

Nyx raised his eyebrows and bent to retrieve the book from the floor.

Other gods came then, blotting the moonlight spilling into the lone window of my favorite room.

Shiloh Raiden, Kansas Raine, Tristan Storme, and Amy Lynn. All the children of Gemini. Full-born gods- born and not made.

"Read it!" I growled, and Shiloh pulled Gi to her knees.

Nyx hurried to open the journal with shaky hands; his lips moved as he read the words. "Gi? We knew, but this?"

"I made him perfect. All Raven had to do was accept him and Jaxon would be taken care of when Raven died." Gi frowned, and Shiloh jerked her head back.

"The mess with Jaxon was over money? You don't mate them!" Gaia yelled. She pushed Nyx out of the way and curtsied. "My Lady. What is your judgment?"

"Wait. Where are Raven and Scot?" Chaos asked.

"Gaia's oldest has them trapped in time. The when, I don't know. The where, is the Veil Club," Noir answered.

Chaos pinched the bridge of his nose. "My Lady, what is your judgment?"

Azure pushed around the made gods, and his brothers followed him into the room. "Tar and feathering would work, Mom." He bent down and kissed my cheek.

"Nah, that's too good," Tristan muttered. "Tried to make me her bastard's brother. I'm not a D'Aubine!" he yelled.

"No, my darling," I murmured, watching the gods and goddesses who agreed with me. Never, in my wildest imagination, would I have assumed the made and born gods would agree on anything.

"My Lady?" My Toad and most faithful companion, Pascal, stepped out of the shadows. "If I might?" He spread his hands and continued to speak. "We could strip her majick and send her to a little house in the country. One of my brothers would be more than happy to serve the ex-goddess of Time tea until she breathes her last."

"Make her Human?" Chaos shuddered at the thought and then grinned.

"Sounds fitting," Nyx murmured.

"I agree," Gaia nodded.

I looked at each of my sons' faces to see if they thought it fitting for the woman who murdered their brothers.

Az nodded once as he glared at Gi.

"We agree, Mamie," Shiloh murmured and wrenched Gi's head back. He plunged a blade into her back and growled in her face. "How's it feel?"

The titanium glowed with power when he jerked it out, and Gi slumped to the floor.

"Shall I?" Pascal offered but didn't wait for an answer.

The made gods backed into the hall again, and the born gods shimmered away, leaving me alone.

Hot tears spilled down my cheeks as I eased into my seat again. The journal landed on the coffee table, and the contract disappeared. A breakfast tray replaced it, and the aroma of freshly brewed coffee blanketed the air.

A roll of parchment shimmered into view next, and I picked it up to read.

'Dear Mamie,

It's not as good as Papa's, but I'm the only one with a kitchen at the moment. We love you and will see you soon.

Kansas'

"Love you, Mom," echoed from the mantel.

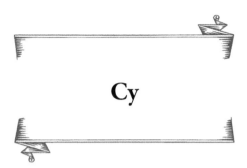

Cy

Lucah paced the living room like his Liger, plotting out loud, his rescue of Raven.

"Wait. Who said you were Raven's mate?" I asked, and Lucah turned, ripped his fly open, and there on his pelvis was a black Feline with red eyes, blinking at me.

Well, damn.

Gods, this was all so messed up. I was Ether, dammit. Me. And I was mated to Raven.

Lucah's eyes narrowed as he watched me. "We'll see about that."

The Veil, the Veil Club, October 31, year indeterminate

R aven
    I hated birthdays.

I ripped James' heart out and tossed it to the ground.

The regret of being born crept in every damned November twenty-eighth.

I didn't need the reminder pounded into my head or have my heart driven out of my chest.

I smiled as my own heart joined the black one ashing away as James grabbed futilely at it to put it back. Well, it was done, and now we'd died together. All the bullshit was over, and I let go. None of it was worth it anymore, and it was time to stop pretending.

Scot fell into me, the bat driving my twin's heart into my chest.

You ready, Brou? I asked.

I'm tired of this shit, my Raven. Oh, good. The bastard is dead.

Our one last act as Justice and War for the world was to obliterate the man's Essence. It exploded around us in a multitude of colors, and the fighting around us stopped to watch the light show. I smiled at Jaxon as the man reached for me. The Light called us home; wherever that was, it wasn't here.

Love was not enough to deal with the fighting anymore, and it couldn't really be love if Jaxon didn't know he would miss me until that moment, could it?

I stumbled when we landed in the middle of an empty dance floor. Scot fell on top of me and pushed to his knees.

It took a minute to focus as I waited for the room to stop spinning.

That's the damned disco ball, Scot grumbled as I carefully pulled the bat out of his back. The glow of eyes from the shadows watched us as we waited to heal, and I felt like the main attraction in a freak show. It was a slow process, but the muscles, bones, nerves, and blood vessels popped back into place. The lungs grew back, and I took a deep breath even before my chest cavity closed again, and I was left with the pink jagged circle over my heart.

Scot patted himself down and then hugged me.

"We're free," he whispered.

"I'd like to know where we are before we make that pronouncement, brother." I waited for someone to step out of the darkness. "I'm Raven Fellideh, and this is my brother Scot."

She? Was six-four with long black hair, Wolf-brown eyes, and a hand on her hip, drawing her silk nightgown tightly across her pelvis to reveal the outline of the dangly bits. "I'm Callie, my lord."

"Not interested." I shook my head and sat down hard.

She laughed, a full throaty sound. "Welcome to The Veil, where it's always Samhain. This is the end of the road, my lords. We are the dead Catori can't kill."

NOTHING BURNS LIKE TIME

... to be continued

Excerpt from Book 2 Madness and Majick

Jace Estienne Corrins

The night before had left me too numb for coherent thought. Was it the Jane Freddie had offered me, the drink that Freddie called Grace, or waking up in a strange bedroom?

Yesterday was my birthday, and Freddie and I had been doing some sort of strange dance for a week. I assumed it was for show. Freddie was the tight end for the football team, with a four-oh GPA and a full scholarship to Geriden's University in the fall. Freddie was a part of the elite crowd of Miss Primm's Preparatory, and never once, in the hours, days, or weeks prior to last week, had the guy even so much looked at me, much less acknowledged my presence.

Miss Primm introduced us the day she gave me my acceptance letter for Geriden's. Frederick Hansen Felix smiled softly in my direction, and nothing more than friendship had ever crossed my mind.

I was a nobody, destined for some lowly position in The Veil's illustrious population of the majickally endowed. I was Human, and under no circumstances did I ever think or wish to be above my station.

Humans were the reason for, and quite beneath, the rest of the population. That knowledge was bred into me from conception, and I accepted my fate. I hoped for a degree and possibly having my own home. Hopefully staying off the Council's radar for the Amans class. I didn't relish the thought of becoming a sex slave to the rich, and if I minded my own business, nobody would try to buy me.

Freddie entered the open bedroom door with a tray and a smile, and those forest-green eyes focused on me.

"Where am I?" I asked as he eased the tray into my lap.

"This is my house. I'm sorry. Do you remember last night?" he asked, and I shook my head, scenting the coffee. Each distinct ingredient was sorted through that action for the first time in my life. The beans were richly roasted, the creamer hinted at vanilla, and three spoons of sugar, all blended together to make the perfect cup.

"Yo, Dee! Where you at?" another male called from somewhere beyond the door before the young man entered.

"Jace, this is JayJay. Uhm, Julian, my brother," Freddie said softly, and worry shimmered away from my friend. No, not friend. More than, but I was still wrapping my brain around breakfast. The eggs were perfectly scrambled, the toast was lightly buttered, and the bread was homemade.

"Nice to meet you," I mumbled and started eating. I wasn't ignoring them exactly; I just didn't have to pay as much attention as I would have the day before.

"I'm going to open the store for Dad this morning," JayJay said, watching me. Freddie wanted his older brother to go away. That thought floated through my head. JayJay knew it, too, but he was curious and waiting for something. I didn't know what he wanted, so I grinned and waved. "Okay, then. I'll just, um, go?" JayJay laughed.

"You do that," Freddie murmured and followed him to the door, closing it with a soft click. I lifted my fork and noticed the bracelet on my right wrist.

Freddie had given it to me the night before, and the stones in the eyes for the Feline pendant glowed as soon as the onyx touched my skin. That, I remembered, but the conversation that followed was still a jumble of sound without syllables.

Memory was a funny thing when laced with... It wasn't the Jane or the Grace. It had been the blood in the Grace that was now slowly revealing the truth. Freddie had been dating me all week on the premise of a scent.

"What did you do?" I whispered, gazing into those fathomless green eyes, and waited for an explanation.

About the Author

Jae Greyn is the author of the Fire Pride Series. Born in the United States, Jae is an advocate for being good humans to animals and people. A consumer of coffee, chocolate, and romances.

Read more at https://jaegreyn.com/.